MIGHTY
Monty

Johanna Hurwitz

illustrated by
Anik McGrory

CANDLEWICK PRESS

For Mighty Ethan
J. H.

For Mighty Meg
A. M.

Text copyright © 2008 by Johanna Hurwitz
Illustrations copyright © 2008 by Anik Scannell McGrory

First paperback edition 2010

The Library of Congress has cataloged the hardcover edition as follows:
Hurwitz, Johanna
Mighty Monty / Johanna Hurwitz ; illustrated by Anik McGrory. —1st ed.
p. cm.
Summary: Monty, a quiet first-grader, continues to come into his own—playing the part of a tree in a miscued school play, sharing his enthusiasm for ants at an outdoor birthday party, and even signing up for karate class despite his asthma.
ISBN 978-0-7636-2977-9 (hardcover)
[1. Asthma—Fiction. 2. Self-confidence—Fiction 3. Schools—Fiction.]
I. McGrory, Anik, ill. II. Title.
PZ7.H9574 Mi 2008
[E]—dc22   2008933496

ISBN 978-0-7636-4786-5 (paperback)

10 11 12 13 14 15 RRC 10 9 8 7 6 5 4 3 2 1

Printed in Crawfordsville, IN, U.S.A.

This book was typeset in Stempel Schneidler.
The illustrations were done in watercolor.

Candlewick Press
99 Dover Street
Somerville, Massachusetts 02144

visit us at www.candlewick.com

Contents

✿

1

Too Much to Read

Montgomery Gerald Morris sounds like the name of a mighty and important person. But Montgomery Gerald Morris was the name of a quiet first-grader who was known to his family and classmates as Monty.

Still, even though he was shy and small, Monty was a mighty smart kid. He was an A+ reader. There were students in sixth grade who couldn't read as well as he could.

In addition to books, Monty liked to read magazines. Magazines had loads of pictures, more than books. So liking magazines as much as he did, you can imagine how excited he was when his next-door neighbor offered him a stack of old magazines.

Mrs. Carlton had been getting ready to sell her house for several months now. She had been cleaning out her basement and attic and garage.

The magazines that Mrs. Carlton showed Monty seemed very interesting. Some were bright yellow with the table of contents right on the cover. Others had a bright yellow border. Monty opened a couple of the magazines and looked inside. They were all filled with page after page of articles and wonderful photographs about everything in the world. This was perfect for Monty because he was interested in lots of things: animals, foreign countries, inventions, and history, just to name a few.

"Thank you very much," said Monty politely as he took the half dozen magazines that his neighbor offered him. He couldn't wait to take them home and begin reading.

"Would you like some more?" asked Mrs. Carlton.

"Sure," said Monty. "Do you have more?"

"Yes, I do," said Mrs. Carlton. "You can have them all."

"Neat," said Monty. "Thank you very much."

"Most of them are in the other room," she said, pointing toward the back of the house. "It will be a big job for you to carry all of them by yourself. Get your dad to help you. I don't want you to overexert yourself."

Monty knew that his neighbor was thinking about his asthma. It was a condition that he had been born with. It meant that sometimes he had trouble breathing and he had to be careful not to bring on an attack. Most of the time, however, he felt fine.

Monty didn't think it was a good idea to ask his father for help. He might just say that Monty didn't need so many magazines. But if he could manage to get them into his house on his own, perhaps his father, and mother too, would be more accepting.

"I'll ask my friend Joey Thomas to help me," said Monty.

"Well, I'll save the magazines for you. Come back when it's convenient." Mrs. Carlton paused a minute. "There's just one thing," she said.

Monty felt disappointed. He had a feeling that Mrs. Carlton was going to ask him to pay for the magazines. He only had two dollars and seventy-three cents saved in his bank.

However, Mrs. Carlton didn't want money. Instead, she surprised Monty by saying, "If you take the magazines, I don't want them back."

"What do you mean?" asked Monty.

"I'm cleaning out this house. Once something goes out, I don't want it to come back in again. So if you take the magazines, they're yours. You can read them or give them away. Just don't bring them back here."

"Okay," agreed Monty. He thought Mrs. Carlton was being silly. Why would he want to bring them back?

In school the next day, Monty saw his friend Joey. "Would you help me carry some old magazines from my next-door neighbor's house over to my house?" he asked shyly. Maybe Joey wouldn't want to bother with Mrs. Carlton's old magazines, he thought. Maybe he was busy with plans of his own.

But Joey was good-natured. "Sure," he agreed at once. "I don't have soccer practice today, so I'll come over as soon as I walk my dogs."

Monty smiled happily. He could hardly wait to get the magazines with Joey's help.

When Monty got home from school, he saw his mother sitting at her sewing machine in the corner of the dining room. She stopped sewing and turned around to face Monty. "I'm making new slipcovers for the chairs in the living room," she said. "Help yourself to an apple from the fruit bowl."

Monty dropped his backpack and went to

get an apple. "Joey and I are going to be busy," he said. "I'm going to get those magazines that I told you about from Mrs. Carlton."

"That's nice," called his mom over the sound of the sewing machine.

Joey met Monty in front of Mrs. Carlton's house. The older woman opened the door when Monty rang her bell. She led the two boys inside.

The sight of the yellow magazines shocked both Monty and Joey. There were many more than Monty had imagined. They were stacked in huge piles as tall as the boys.

"You sure like to read," said Joey to the elderly woman.

"Actually, my husband used to read these," said Mrs. Carlton. "You are looking at more than fifty years' worth of magazines."

"Fifty years!" both boys exclaimed. Fifty years seemed like an awfully long, long time. Fifty years ago was like something Monty would read about in a history book.

"That's fifty times twelve," said Monty with amazement. He was much better at reading than at math so he couldn't figure out the answer in his head. Neither could Joey. But they could see that fifty times twelve was a lot of magazines. Each boy took an armload and walked with them out of Mrs. Carlton's house. Joey was stronger than Monty, so his armload was twice the size of Monty's. Monty wished he was as strong as his friend. Still, he realized, he was lucky to have a friend with strong muscles. Maybe, he fantasized, someday in the future, he,

Monty Gerald Morris, would develop the might of a superhero. He'd be Mighty Monty then.

"Where do you want to put them?" Joey asked, breaking into Monty's daydream.

"Up in my room," said Monty. As he spoke, he stopped to figure out where they would all fit. He could put some under his bed and make a tall pile by his chest of drawers. The boys walked into Monty's house and up the stairs to his room. Monty started a pile by the chest, and Joey added his armload on top. Then they went downstairs and returned to Mrs. Carlton's house.

On the fourth trip, Monty's mother called out above the motor of her sewing machine, "Is everything all right, you guys?"

"Yes, fine," said Monty, stopping to catch his breath. He was getting tired from going up and down stairs. He was beginning to worry too. His room was getting very crowded. He didn't think his mother would be pleased. On the other hand, she always said reading was important. So maybe it wouldn't be a problem after all.

An hour later, Monty was exhausted and his room was filled with magazines. They were in two tall piles on either side of the chest of drawers. There were also magazines under his bed and on the floor of his closet and on top of the chest and lying sideways on his bookshelf. And there was a pile behind the bedroom door and another by the window.

Monty and Joey sat down on Monty's bed. "This looks like a magazine store," said Joey, looking around in amazement. "I never ever saw so many magazines in my life."

"Me either," said Monty. "I guess I'm going to be very busy reading them all."

"You won't have any time to play or anything," commented Joey.

Monty tried to count the magazines. But there were so many that he kept getting confused. "I have hundreds of magazines," he finally decided.

"I never had hundreds of anything," said Joey.

"Me either," said Monty.

Joey shrugged. "I'm getting hungry," he said. "I think it must be time for me to go home for supper."

"Okay," agreed Monty. He was feeling pretty hungry too after all his work.

He went downstairs with Joey. Mrs. Morris was putting all her sewing away. "Have a good time this afternoon?" she asked, smiling at the boys.

"Yes," said Monty.

Mrs. Morris went into the kitchen to prepare supper. Monty went back up to his room. He had homework to do, and he thought he ought to begin reading his magazines. It might take him the rest of his life to finish them all.

But before he could read even the first one, his father came home. Mr. Morris poked his head in Monty's room and stopped, stunned. "What in the world is all this?" he asked.

"Magazines," said Monty.

"I can see they're magazines, but where did they come from?"

"Mrs. Carlton gave them to me."

Mr. Morris could hardly open the door to walk into the room. Then he accidentally bumped into one of the tall stacks of magazines. Of course they all went tumbling to the floor and caused a tremendous noise. That was because there was no carpeting on the wood floors. The floors were bare because the lint from carpeting was not good for Monty's asthma.

"There are too many magazines in here," said Mr. Morris as he stooped to pick up a few of them. "You had better bring some of them back to her."

"Okay," Monty agreed without arguing. He'd known that his parents would not be thrilled by the way his room looked. Then he remembered something. "But Mrs. Carlton said I can't give them back," he told his father.

"What?"

"She said if I took them, they were mine. And she doesn't want them back." Monty paused while he considered the problem. "Maybe we can give them to someone else?"

"Someone who can't give them back to us," said Monty's dad as he bent to pick up some more of the magazines. "Otherwise, we'll just have to put them out with our recycling."

Monty didn't like that idea at all. First, Mrs. Carlton would see her husband's old possessions going into the garbage. And second, it seemed like such a waste of good magazines.

Over supper, Monty's parents discussed who might like receiving six hundred magazines.

"No, not all," Monty said. "Dad told me I could keep some of them."

"You can pick out a dozen," his mother said. She had been doubly shocked when she had seen Monty's room. She was amazed that it had all happened while she was busy sewing. "I didn't notice a thing," she said over and over to her husband.

"Maybe the school library would like them," suggested Monty.

"I don't think the place is big enough for all those magazines," said Mrs. Morris.

"How about the public library?" Monty asked.

"They had a big sign up last fall when they had their annual book sale. It said, *Donations appreciated. But no textbooks or magazines.*"

"What about the senior center?" said Monty.

"They might take some. But no one in the world is going to want fifty years' worth of old magazines."

"I want them," Monty reminded his parents.

"Impossible," said Mrs. Morris firmly. Then, seeing the sad expression on Monty's face, she added, "Besides, you can borrow copies from the library and you can look up lots of that information on the Internet."

In the end, Monty selected, with great, great difficulty, twelve issues of the magazine to keep for himself. Some were donated to the senior center in town and some were donated to another senior center in the neighboring community where Mr. Morris went to work. There were still many, many magazines left.

Then Monty remembered how when he was in preschool, his class used to cut pictures out of magazines. They made alphabet books and looked for items that started with each letter from *A* to *Z*.

"Perfect!" exclaimed Mrs. Morris when Monty reminded her about it. So Monty donated all the leftover magazines to his old preschool. They could make alphabet books and collages with all the pictures. They could cut out pictures for years to come.

The next day, there was just one small pile of twelve yellow magazines in Monty's bedroom.

"Please don't accept any other gifts without checking with us," Monty's mom said.

"Hmmm. All right," said Monty, looking up. He was very absorbed in a fascinating article all about dolphins that was in one of the magazines he had kept for himself. The article had neat pictures. No preschooler would be able to make a *D* is for *Dolphin* page in their alphabet book—they'd have to search for another picture in another magazine.

2

Monty on Stage

Monty's first-grade teacher was named Mrs. Meaney. At the start of the school year, he had been nervous. A name like *Meaney* sounded like it was the name of a very grouchy person.

Monty had been happy to discover that his teacher was not like that at all. Mrs. Meaney smiled a lot and rarely scolded the students. She had loads of good ideas, and she made first grade a great deal of fun. In fact, Monty noticed that she used the word *great* very often when she spoke to the class.

One day she said, "I have some great news for you. Our class is going to put on a play for the other first-grade classes." She smiled. "I bet some of you are great budding actors," she added.

Monty didn't think putting on a play was such great news. He was sure he wasn't a budding actor. Monty was nervous about being in a play. It meant he'd have to stand

on a stage in front of an audience of students, teachers, and parents. Everyone would be looking at him. Suppose he made a mistake. Suppose everyone laughed at him. He'd much rather just be a part of the audience and not an actor at all.

The play was about the environment, and Monty was cast as a tree. "What kind of a tree am I?" he asked anxiously.

"You can be any sort you wish," said Mrs. Meaney, smiling. Then she changed her mind. "You can't be a palm tree, however. There are no palm trees around here."

Monty didn't mind. He'd only seen pictures of palm trees or seen them in movies. He'd pick a different tree. But he wished he didn't have to be a tree at all.

Mrs. Meaney gave out the other parts. One student was the rain. Another was the sun. Still others represented a river, birds, insects, and the wind. Three girls in Monty's class who were also very shy were going to be flowers. They would speak their lines together, which was less scary than standing in front of everyone and speaking out all alone.

Monty raised his hand. "I'm an apple tree," he announced.

"Great," said Mrs. Meaney. "I love apples. We need lots of apple trees in the world."

Monty learned his part: "Trees are important. They give us shade; they give us wood; they give us fruit. Their roots hold water in the soil, and their limbs provide homes for birds."

Although Monty quickly learned his lines, he couldn't always remember what the rain and the sun and the flowers had to say.

Often during rehearsals, the students got confused and spoke at the wrong time. Some forgot to speak at all.

"I have a great plan," said Mrs. Meaney. "It will make being in this play very easy for everyone. All you each need to remember is the last word of the person who speaks before you. Their last word will be the cue for when to start reciting your part.

Don't speak until you hear your special word."

The student who spoke before Monty was Cora Rose. She was the land. Her last line was "The land provides a home for plants and trees."

"When you hear the word *trees,* you'll know that it's your turn to speak," Mrs. Meaney told Monty. "Don't say anything until you hear the word *trees,*" she repeated.

Not only did the children learn their parts; they also made costumes out of large sheets of paper. Monty cut his paper into the shape of a tree. He cut little holes in the tree trunk. That way, he could hold the paper tree up in front of him and peek through the holes at the audience. He colored the tree trunk a dark brown, and he put leaves on its branches.

Then he cut out circles, which he colored red, and pasted them onto the branches. Those were the apples on his tree. The best thing about his costume was that he was hiding behind it when he spoke.

The students held a dress rehearsal the day before the play. Each one held their costume up in front of himself or herself. Cora Rose, who was the land, had a costume that looked like a map. It was so big that Mrs. Meaney helped her make holes and tie string through them. That way, Cora Rose could put the string over her head and her costume hung down, covering all of her body except her head.

Monty listened when Cora spoke. As always, her last line was "The land provides the homes for plants and trees." As soon as he heard the word *trees,* he stepped forward, peeking out of his costume, and began speaking.

"You are all great!" said Mrs. Meaney enthusiastically. "You'll do a great job tomorrow. I'm so proud of all of you."

The next afternoon, Monty's parents both came to see the play. They sat in the back of the school auditorium with all the other parents who had managed to come to the school. Mrs. Meaney's class giggled nervously. Everyone knew their parts. Everyone's costume was ready.

Even though the day before he had felt a bit more confident, now that it was time for the play to begin, Monty felt scared all over again. Because of his asthma, Monty always carried a special device called an inhaler in his pocket. It helped him breathe if he felt he was getting an asthma attack. It was comforting to have. Now, feeling nervous about the play, Monty put his hand in his pocket and touched the inhaler.

He wasn't the only one who felt scared. "I'm nervous," Cora complained.

"That's great," said Mrs. Meaney.

"It is?" asked Patricia. It seemed a strange answer from the teacher.

"Of course. It's great to be nervous. That means you are also excited, and it means you'll give a great performance. In show business they always say, 'Break a leg.'"

"That's a mean thing to tell someone," said Cora.

"It sounds mean, but they really are wishing the actors good luck."

One of his classmates poked Monty. "Break a leg," he said.

Monty turned to the three flowers who were standing nearby. "Break a leg," he told them. "Break three legs. Break six legs."

"Shhh," Mrs. Meaney told the students. "The play is about to begin."

Monty's friend Joey Thomas was the narrator. He didn't have a paper costume. Instead, he was wearing a shirt with a necktie and a jacket. It made him look important, but Monty was glad he had a paper tree trunk to hide behind. Joey began: "The environment is very important. We must all work to keep it clean and . . ."

Monty stopped listening. He had heard all these words too many times. Instead, he peeked through his tree holes and smiled when he saw his parents. He recognized some of the other parents in the back of the room too.

The rain spoke and so did the wind. Monty watched for the land. Cora moved

toward the front of the stage. "The land provides a home for plants," she said.

She didn't say anything about trees. Monty listened. He didn't hear the word *trees,* so he didn't speak. He stood holding his paper tree trunk with one hand and put his other hand in his pocket to feel the inhaler. "Go on, go on," the flowers urged Monty.

"I can't," Monty whispered as he clutched the inhaler. "She didn't say *trees.*"

"Say *trees,*" someone whispered to Cora.

Cora had moved to the rear of the stage.

With prodding from her classmates, she ran forward and called out, "Trees!" in a loud voice. Then she ran to the rear of the stage again.

Now Monty knew it was time for him to begin.

"Trees are important," he shouted to the audience from behind his paper tree trunk. "They give us shade; they give us wood; they give us fruit. Their roots hold water in the soil."

Monty sighed with relief. He had said his lines. The only problem was, like Cora before him, he had forgotten the line with the cue word for the next actor. He didn't say the word *birds,* and Todd, who was waiting to say his part, couldn't go on. For the second time, the play came to a halt.

"Say *birds,*" Mrs. Meaney called softly to Monty.

Monty stood in the center of the stage. He couldn't remember what he was supposed to say about birds. He began his little speech again. "Trees are important. They give us shade; they give us wood; they give us fruit. Their roots hold water in the soil, and their

limbs provide homes for BIRDS." He shouted the last word extra loudly and with relief. At last he was finished and he could move to the back of the stage.

Todd, who was a blue jay, could begin to recite his part.

As the play progressed, some of the other students forgot to give the cue words just as Cora and Monty had done. The play wasn't turning out exactly the way Mrs. Meaney had planned it.

At the very end of the performance, the teacher came forward. She hadn't given herself a part in the play, but she spoke anyhow. "Just as some of the parts were forgotten, that is how we have been treating our environment. We must not forget to conserve our resources. The environment is important for all of us and for our children too," she said. Then she began clapping, which was a signal for the audience to join in too.

"I think Mrs. Meaney's going to have a baby," Monty whispered, above the sound of the applause, to Todd, who was standing next to him. "Did you hear what she said about 'our children'?"

"So's my mom," Todd said.

"Mrs. Meaney's going to be a mom," said someone else.

"When are you going to have your baby?" Ilene Kelly asked the teacher.

Mrs. Meaney looked surprised. "Who said I'm going to have a baby?" she asked.

The students looked around to see who had started the rumor. "You said we need to take care of the environment for our children," Monty remembered.

"I meant everybody's children," Mrs. Meaney explained. "I'm not having a baby," she said. "But you are all my children. Now we're going to go back to the classroom and have a little party to celebrate the great job you did with this play."

Everyone in the class had the same reaction. "Great!"

"You know what else is great?" asked Monty.

"What?" asked Mrs. Meaney.

"Even if we forgot some of our words, nobody broke a leg."

"That *is* great. I think I have a class full of budding actors," said Mrs. Meaney, smiling at them all.

3

Monty Joins a Class

Monty knew he was not a budding actor. Neither was he a budding athlete or a budding singer. But he thought that if he took some sort of special after-school class, like most of the other kids in the first grade, he might develop some new skills. Maybe he would become something besides just plain Monty.

For example, Joey Thomas and Paul Freeman were on a soccer team, and Cora Rose took a ballet class. Monty could go on and on thinking of all the after-school activities in which his classmates participated.

"Can't I take a special class after school?" Monty asked his mother. "I'd like to be on the soccer team with Joey."

"I don't want you to overexert yourself," said Mrs. Morris. "You've been doing so well. You haven't had a bad asthma attack in months. Let's see if we can keep this up."

"It's not fair," said Monty. "I bet I could do something."

"Piano lessons wouldn't tire you out," said Mrs. Morris. "But we don't have a piano. I think you'd need one for practicing."

"I don't want to take piano lessons," said

Monty. "I want to take a class with other kids."

"That eliminates all sorts of music lessons," said his mother.

"I want a sport," said Monty.

"Absolutely not. I told you. Soccer is out. Little League baseball is out. Ice hockey, lacrosse—those are all sports that you just can't do. Maybe when you get older," she added to make Monty feel better.

It didn't work. Monty didn't feel better thinking that when he was older he could do things like other kids. He wanted to do something now. Then one day, the twins Arlene and Ilene, who lived on his street, told him about their karate lessons.

"Karate?" asked Monty, impressed. "Isn't that when you learn how to throw people to the ground so they won't beat you up?"

"It does teach us self-defense," said Ilene, "but we don't spend all our time throwing each other down. It's lots of fun, and we're learning all sorts of good things."

"Like what?" asked Monty. He was getting curious.

The two sisters began listing all they'd learned. "Respect, love, peace, joy," Arlene recited.

"Don't forget self-control, discipline, trust, integrity . . ." Ilene added.

"How can you learn so much?" asked Monty. "There won't be any time left for self-defense."

"There's time for everything," said Ilene. "We've only gone for a few months and already we know lots of movements."

"And it's lots of fun. We get to wear this

special white uniform. And we have yellow belts already," said Arlene.

"The color of your belt changes the better you get," Ilene explained.

The more the girls told him about their after-school karate class, the more it interested Monty.

"You could come and be in our class," Arlene told Monty. "It has boys and girls."

Monty thought about it. He wanted to take karate lessons, but he was a bit scared of doing it too. Maybe he wouldn't be able to keep up with the other students.

"Arlene and Ilene take karate lessons," he told his parents that evening when they were eating supper. "Can I?"

"Karate? I'm not sure that's something you

could do," said Mrs. Morris. "It's probably much too strenuous."

"Arlene and Ilene don't look very athletic to me," commented Mr. Morris thoughtfully. "I remember when their father was teaching them how to ride their bikes. I thought it would be easier to teach a pair of dogs than to teach those girls."

Monty giggled. He remembered how the sisters had fallen off their bikes so many times. Their father was the one who did the strenuous part until they finally learned to balance themselves.

"Could you take me to watch?" suggested Monty. "Maybe I won't even like it. But maybe I would. And maybe it would be okay for me. Ilene said the kids in the class are all ages, from five to ten."

"That sounds reasonable," agreed Mr. Morris, looking at his wife. "We shouldn't rule it out until we've actually seen what it's all about."

So the following Tuesday, Mrs. Morris took Monty to the karate school and Mr. Morris met them there. The three of them sat in the back of the large practice room with some of the parents of class members. Arlene and Ilene and about eight other students took their places. The children all had white outfits on, and most of them had yellow belts tied around their waists like the twins. But one small boy had a white belt and one tall girl had an orange belt. Their teacher stood in front wearing a black belt.

"Good afternoon," he called out to the children. He bowed toward them.

"Good afternoon, sir," they responded in unison. They bowed to the teacher.

"Ten jumping jacks," he called out.

"Yes, sir!" the students shouted. Then the boys and girls all began jumping up and down and waving their arms.

"I could do that," Monty whispered to his parents. "It's easy. We do that at school too."

"If ten was too many, they'd probably let him stop at half a dozen," Mr. Morris told his wife.

"Ten push-ups," called the teacher when the students had completed their jumping.

"Yes, sir."

Monty and his parents watched all the activities. "I could do that," Monty whispered over and over again. It really looked like fun, and he hoped his parents would agree that he could join the class. Sometimes the students shouted out as they moved. It sounded like they were saying "Kee-yi!" Monty thought he'd have to ask Arlene and Ilene to tell him what it meant.

"Those kicks are just like ballet steps," commented Monty's mother when the students were instructed to point their toes out and lift their feet.

When the class was over, Monty's parents went to speak with the teacher. The twins had told Monty that he was called Sensei Jack. "*Sensei* means 'teacher,'" Ilene had explained to him. Monty stood nearby listening as his parents talked about his interest and their concern. "We don't want to endanger his health," said Mrs. Morris.

"But we don't want him to be deprived of activities," Mr. Morris said.

The *sensei* nodded. Then he pointed to all the goals of karate that were listed on signs around the room. "Just as the students strive to learn all of these attributes, so must I obey them too. I must respect my students and their limitations. I must honor their needs with sincerity and love. And you must trust me," he said, smiling at Monty's parents.

The teacher turned to look at Monty.

"What do you think, young man? Would you like to join our class?"

"Oh, yes," said Monty eagerly.

"What?" demanded the *sensei*.

For a moment, Monty wondered if the karate teacher was hard of hearing. Then he remembered how the students spoke to him.

"Yes, sir," he said, standing up very straight and looking the teacher in the eye.

"This boy is a fast learner," said the *sensei*. "That's good."

"Let's give it a try," suggested Mr. Morris. "Can we sign up for a limited trial period? Say two or three months?"

"A good plan," the teacher agreed. "Come," he directed Monty. He walked over to a cabinet and opened it. He measured Monty with his eyes and then pulled out a white karate outfit of cotton pants and a matching jacket. Next he handed Monty a white belt.

"You will start with this belt," he told Monty.

"Yes, sir," Monty responded to the *sensei*.

Afterward, at home, Monty said to his parents, "I don't care if I don't have a yellow belt like Arlene and Ilene. White is my favorite color."

"It is?" asked his mother. "That's news to me."

"Sure," said Monty. "White is the color of snow. And it's the color of vanilla ice cream, and mashed potatoes, and marshmallows. Those are all great things. I love white."

Monty's father smiled at his son. "Yes, sir."

Monty was excited to start studying karate. He looked forward to Thursday, when he would accompany Arlene and Ilene to the class. Before he went to bed, he tried on his white outfit in front of the mirror and admired himself. He looked just like all the students. He practiced tying his white belt the special way that Sensei had shown him.

But at four thirty on Thursday afternoon, when Monty stood with the other students waiting for the karate teacher, he began to feel nervous. It had seemed like such a good idea to take karate lessons when he was at home. Now he wondered why he had been so eager. Maybe he wouldn't be able to keep up with the other kids. Maybe they would laugh at him when he tried to do what they did.

Monty wiggled his toes on the bare wood floor. He looked down at them. They looked as if they belonged at the beach or in the bathtub. His toes were not used to being exposed in a class situation. They seemed to miss their socks and shoes. Monty moved his hand in search of a pocket. There were no pockets in his uniform. That meant that he didn't have his inhaler close at hand because there was nowhere for it to stay. Monty shuddered slightly. He was not used to being without his special breathing device.

"Are you cold?" Arlene whispered to him. She was standing nearby. "You'll warm up in a minute when we start doing the jumping jacks."

Monty nodded. It was too complicated to explain that he wasn't cold. He was scared.

Just then the teacher walked to the front of the room.

"Good afternoon," he called out to the students. He bowed toward them.

"Good afternoon, sir," everyone responded. They bowed back to their instructor.

"Ten jumping jacks," he told them.

"Yes, sir," Monty and the other students called out. Then they began the jumping.

Monty kept count: one, two, three . . . He was pleased to see that he could reach ten just like the others.

Push-ups were harder. By the third one, he was out of breath.

He sat on the floor, watching the students. He worried that the teacher would throw him out of the class, but Sensei did not seem to notice him.

"All the way down, Mike," the teacher called out to one of the boys.

"Yes, sir," a boy's voice rang out.

"If you don't do a real push-up, I'll have to assign more," the teacher warned.

One or two voices called out, "Aww."

"What did I hear?" asked the teacher.

"Yes, sir," the students shouted.

"Sir, that boy isn't doing his push-ups," a voice called out.

Monty blushed with embarrassment. He didn't know who had told on him, but he knew he was the boy not doing the push-ups.

"That's no concern of yours," the teacher said sharply. "Do an extra five push-ups for calling out."

"Yes, sir."

As Monty managed to do a couple more push-ups, he was sure that whoever had told on him, and was assigned the extra ones, was going to hate him.

"First position," the *sensei* called out when the students had completed the push-ups.

Monty watched and copied the students around him.

"Eyes forward. Arms outstretched," the *sensei* commanded.

"Yes, sir."

Monty began to realize that although the *sensei* seemed very strict when he shouted his commands, he was teasing and joking with his students at the same time.

Sometimes the students and teacher let out loud cries. When they were doing a forefist punch, the students called out, "Kee-yi!"

Monty was startled by the loud cries around him.

"Again!" shouted Sensei Jack.

Again the students extended their arms and, with fists down, called out, "Kee-yi!"

Monty's cry came out as a little squeak, and he blushed. He was not used to shouting in a classroom. However, by his fourth attempt at the forefist punch, he heard himself shout just as loudly as his classmates.

By the end of the class, Monty discovered that he had forgotten about his inhaler. He hadn't really needed it at all. His bare toes skipped into the changing room to put on his socks and shoes.

Monty's mom was waiting to pick up Arlene and Ilene and him. She looked at Monty and pushed the hair from his eyes. "How are you feeling?" she asked as he got into the car.

"Fine," he assured her. And he really was fine.

And so a new routine was set up: Every Tuesday and Thursday, Monty and the twins went off to karate class. Mrs. Kelly, the twins' mother, drove them to the class. Monty's mother brought them back home. After a few weeks, the karate teacher took Monty aside and tested him. Monty showed how he had quickly learned the basic karate positions.

"Good work," said Sensei Jack. He presented Monty with a yellow belt.

"Look," Monty showed his mother with pride when she came to pick the kids up. "I don't have a white belt anymore. I've been promoted to yellow."

"But white is your favorite color," said Mrs. Morris.

"Oh, no," Monty said, shaking his head. "Yellow is my favorite color."

"It is?"

"Sure. Yellow is the color of sunshine and daffodils and lemon meringue pie and the covers of the magazines that I got from Mrs. Carlton."

"You're right," agreed Mrs. Morris. "Those things are all yellow."

"It gets harder and harder to move on to the next color belt," Arlene warned Monty. "We've been yellow a long time. But we keep practicing so we'll get the next color."

"How many colors are there?" asked Monty's mother.

"White, yellow, orange, purple, green,

blue, red, brown, black," the two sisters recited in unison.

"Black is the best," said Arlene.

Black might be the best for other people, but Monty was mighty happy to have been given a yellow belt. And he looked forward to wearing it on the following Tuesday and Thursday afternoons. After all, yellow was his favorite color.

4

Joey's Birthday Party

One day Monty got a letter in the mail. It was an invitation to his friend Joey's birthday party. Since Joey lived just halfway up the other side of the street, he could have easily handed the invitation to Monty. Or he could have just asked him without a printed card. But Monty was glad to get an invitation in the mail. First-grade boys don't get many letters, so it was special to have it waiting on the kitchen table when he came home from school. That was the good news.

The bad news was that the party, which was next Saturday, would take place in Joey's house. Monty had never been inside Joey's house because his friend owned not one, but two, dogs. Monty's asthma was always made worse by close contact with dogs and cats.

"Couldn't I go anyway?" Monty begged his mom.

"It's not a good idea," said Mrs. Morris, shaking her head. "You'll just have to explain to Joey that you can't go. He knows about your allergic reaction to his dogs."

Monty felt miserable. What good was a birthday invitation if you couldn't attend the party? What good was having a friend if you couldn't ever visit his house?

Joey was disappointed too when Monty told him the news.

"My mom says I'll still give you a present," Monty said.

Joey smiled. "That's good. But I still wish you could come. I invited seven boys because it's my seventh birthday. And we're going to have lunch and play loads of games."

"I bet it will be lots of fun," said Monty. "What's for lunch?"

"Hamburgers and French fries. And afterward, ice-cream cake. My mom is getting a chocolate one that we saw in a store."

"It sounds delicious," said Monty. He sighed. He imagined all the boys playing together and then eating the birthday food. He loved ice-cream cake. Suddenly he had an idea. "Could I sit on the steps outside your house and eat the lunch there? I wouldn't be able to come inside and play, but at least I could have the birthday lunch." It would probably be terrible sitting outside all alone. But he would do it anyway. It would be better than nothing.

"Sure," said Joey. "I know my mom will say yes to that." Joey began working out the details. "We can bring your food outside. And we can open the window so you can sing

'Happy Birthday' to me." Joey thought it would work out just fine.

But when Joey's mother heard about the plan, she disagreed. "I'm so sorry that I forgot about your allergy," she told Monty. "I don't want you sitting outside by yourself. We'll just hold the party outdoors. Then you won't miss any of the fun."

Monty smiled. Now he wouldn't be weird celebrating Joey's birthday outdoors while everyone else was in the house.

"What happens if it rains?" asked Joey suddenly. It was an awful thought.

Luckily it didn't rain on Saturday. Promptly at twelve thirty, Monty crossed the street and went over to Joey's house. He was holding a gift-wrapped package. It was a board game about going on a safari hunt. As he arrived at

Joey's house, a car pulled up, and two boys jumped out. Monty recognized them from school. They were Todd and Danny. They were each holding birthday presents too. As they stood looking at each other, still another boy arrived. He had a wrapped gift too.

"Are you going to Joey's birthday party?" Todd asked.

"Yep. My name is Clifford. I'm on the soccer team with Joey."

"Hi," Monty greeted Clifford. "Did you know the party is outdoors?" he asked the boys. "That's because of Joey's dogs."

"That's weird," said Danny. "What do you mean 'because of the dogs'?"

"I can't go inside because I'm allergic to dog hair."

"Yuck," said Danny. "I'm glad I'm not allergic to dogs.

"I'm not allergic to dogs," said Clifford, "but I can't eat peanuts. I'm allergic to them."

"It's good you're not a squirrel," said Danny as the door opened.

Joey greeted his friends. "Come around the back," he said. "We're going to play some games before lunch."

Joey's father organized a game of Simon Says.

Monty stood next to Clifford and raised his arms and clapped his hands according to the instructions. Before long, however, he'd been tricked into doing the wrong thing and so he went and sat on a lawn chair and watched the others. In the end, it was Danny who won the game.

The next game was Hot Potato. The boys stood in a circle, throwing a real potato to one another while Joey's father turned a CD player on and off. When the music stopped, whoever was holding the potato was out. Monty was the first one out. He just wasn't very good at these party games. Still, he was awfully glad to be part of the party.

He sat down again and waited for the game to be over. He retied the lace on his left sneaker. Then, because he had nothing else to do, he retied the lace on his right sneaker. He saw an ant walking near his right foot. Monty watched as the ant slowly moved across the step.

"Do you know that you are at a party?" Monty whispered to the ant.

The ant kept walking. Amazingly, he joined up with several others. It looked as if the ants were holding a party of their own.

Danny came over to Monty. "These are baby games," he complained. Monty guessed he was unhappy to be out so quickly.

"You can't win every game," Monty said.

"Why not?" grumbled Danny as he walked away. "I'm bored."

Monty began to worry that the party would have been more fun if it was indoors. It would be his fault if others like Danny weren't having a good time.

When the game of Hot Potato ended, Joey's mother came out with a tray of hamburgers and buns. "Everyone, rinse your hands off," she said, pointing to a hose nearby. Washing and splashing were more fun than any party games. A lot more than hands got wet, but the sun was shining and it didn't matter.

"I'm starving," said Clifford to Monty.

"Me too," Monty agreed. All the boys took seats around the table.

Suddenly the seven guests and Joey were silent. Everyone was busy chewing on the birthday hamburgers and drinking lemonade.

When he was almost finished eating, Monty remembered the ants. He wondered what they ate for lunch. He broke off a piece of his hamburger roll and looked down at his feet. Sure enough, after a moment of searching, he saw an ant moving by. "Do ants like hamburgers?" he whispered to the ant.

He broke the roll into small pieces and scattered them at his feet, then proceeded to finish eating. By the time he had eaten the last of his meal, he saw one of the ants investigating the crumbs.

Monty held his breath. Would the ant pick it up and carry it away?

"What are you looking at?" Clifford leaned over and asked Monty

"You want to see something neat?" Monty responded.

"Sure."

Monty pointed out the crumbs and the ants. One of the ants was walking away carrying a tiny piece of the hamburger roll.

"Wow," said Clifford. He sat down on the ground to get a closer look at the ants.

"What are you doing?" Joey asked Clifford and Monty.

"We're watching the ants."

Joey bent to examine the ants. "Cool," he said.

Todd came over next. "What are you doing?" he asked.

"Look," said Joey.

Todd bent to look as now three ants were carting away bread crumbs.

"I'll get them," said Todd, raising his foot to stamp on the ants.

"No!" shouted Monty, and he found himself blocking Todd's foot with his leg. It wasn't exactly a karate move, but it was close.

Todd lost his balance and fell to the ground with a thud. "What did you do that for?" he demanded. "They're just old bugs."

"They have a right to live too," said Monty.

"Yeah," agreed Clifford and Joey together.

All the boys had finished eating by now. "What are you doing?" asked one of them. "Can we play too?"

"We're not playing. We're watching these little ants," said Joey, pointing to the insects crawling across the ground.

"Boys," Joey's mother called out. She'd been clearing the plates and cups from the table. "It's time to play some more games."

"Yuck," said Danny.

"Do we have to play games?" asked Joey. "This is more fun. Monty found some ants, and they're really interesting to watch."

"These ants are very smart," said Todd, who was now admiring the same insects that he'd tried to smash just a few minutes before.

"Well, what about the birthday cake?" asked Joey's mom. "Don't you want to have your cake?"

Of course everyone wanted birthday cake.

In a couple of minutes, Mrs. Thomas returned carrying a platter with the ice-cream cake. Behind her followed Mr. Thomas. He held a pile of paper plates and plastic spoons.

Eight candles were in the cake: seven were for each year of Joey's life and one to grow on. Mr. Thomas lit the candles, and the boys all sang "Happy Birthday."

After Joey blew out the candles, his mom began cutting slices of cake for everyone.

"It's chocolate," said Todd. "I can't eat chocolate. I'm allergic to it."

"It's made of ice cream," said Danny. "I'm allergic to milk and anything made with milk."

"I'm glad there are no peanuts in the cake," said Clifford. "Remember, I told you that I'm allergic to peanuts," he said to Monty.

Monty happily ate his slice of ice-cream cake while Joey's mom ran back into the house. She returned carrying a box of vanilla cookies that weren't made with chocolate, milk, or peanuts. Monty had a second slice of cake because it appeared there was more than enough to go around since not everyone could eat it. Having asthma wasn't good,

Monty thought. But at least he could still eat chocolate and ice cream and peanuts. He felt really sorry for the boys who had those allergies. He looked at them. Todd and Danny were eating the cookies and watching the ants. They even made a few cookie crumbs for the ants so they could celebrate Joey's birthday too. It was like having lots of extra guests at the party.

"I love watching the ants," said Clifford. "I bet I have some around my house, but I

Monty smiled. He'd worried that he might have ruined the party for Joey because it had to be outdoors. But it hadn't rained and it had turned out to be wonderful. He was sure glad that he'd been able to come. No one is ever allergic to having a good time.

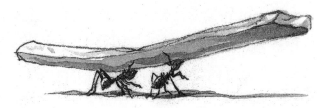

never noticed them before." He turned to Monty. "It's great that you showed them to us."

The planned party games were forgotten as the eight boys crawled about on their hands and knees watching the ants. It was even better when Mrs. Thomas remembered something. She went inside the house and returned holding eight magnifying glasses, one for each. "These were in the goody bags," she explained. "Isn't that lucky?"

5

The Karate Exhibition

Before he knew it, Monty had been taking karate classes twice a week for several weeks. A little while after he joined the class, there had been an exhibition. It took place in the evening, after supper, and that had made it extra special.

Because Monty was a new student, he had not taken part. Instead, he had sat in the back of the room with Arlene and Ilene's parents. All around them were other parents, siblings, and friends of the participants. Monty had been excited to watch the students show off their skills. Someday he would be able to do all the things that they did. Still, he was relieved just to be sitting in the back. He didn't like to have lots of people watching him. He watched Arlene and Ilene and the other classmates perform. At the end of the evening, both girls had been awarded new belts as a sign that they had improved their skills significantly. They showed off their orange belts proudly to Monty. And on the way home, Mr. Kelly stopped at the ice-cream stand in town and bought everyone a double-scooped cone to celebrate his daughters' achievement.

Now it was time for another exhibition. This time Monty was expected to participate with the other karate students.

"Aren't you excited?" Ilene asked Monty. "It's so much fun to go to the karate school at night."

Monty shrugged. He wasn't excited about the exhibition at all.

"Can't I just watch like last time?" Monty asked Sensei.

"You have been progressing nicely," the teacher said. "Don't you want your parents to see how well you can perform?"

"They see me at home all the time," Monty told the teacher. "I show them when I practice my positions and kicks."

"Good," said Sensei, nodding. "Then you won't be even a little bit nervous during the exhibition. You're used to having an audience."

Sensei was right, and Sensei was wrong. Monty was not a little bit nervous on the evening of the exhibition. He was a lot nervous.

Arlene and Ilene had told Joey about the exhibition. "Can I come with you and watch?" he asked Monty.

"It would be boring for you," Monty said. "You better stay home." He didn't want his friend to come. It would make him more nervous than ever during the exhibition.

As Monty put on his white karate uniform and tied his yellow belt, he thought about the class play earlier in the year. He remembered how nervous he had felt then. But at least

that time, he was able to hide behind his paper tree. This time there was nothing to hide behind. Monty thought about how awful he'd felt when he'd forgotten the last line of his part. No one had seen him blush with embarrassment, but he knew his face had turned very red. This time, if he made a mistake, everyone would see him. And this time, he didn't have a pocket with his inhaler for comfort. He was glad Joey wasn't coming with him.

"I don't feel well," he told his parents in the evening as they were getting ready to leave the house.

Mrs. Morris put her hand to Monty's forehead. "You feel very cool," she said. "You don't have a fever."

"Are you having trouble with your breathing?" asked Monty's father.

Monty knew he was concerned about an asthma attack.

It would have been the easiest thing in the world to say he couldn't breathe. Then his parents would not expect Monty to go to the exhibition. In fact, they would have forbidden his going out at all.

But Monty was honest. He didn't want to upset his parents with worry about his breathing. So he didn't take the easy way out. He shook his head. "I can breathe fine right now," he said softly. "But I think I might have trouble during the exhibition. I just wish I could stay home and not be in the exhibition at all."

"Oh, Monty, you have stage fright," said his father, smiling.

"Well, I can't have stage fright. There isn't a stage," Monty argued.

"That's true. But it would still be considered a form of stage fright. What's the worst thing that could happen?" Mr. Morris asked his son.

"I could do something stupid. I could kick the wrong way. Or I could shout out at the wrong time. People would laugh at me."

"No way," said his father. "There are all those signs around the room reminding people about respect and consideration. No one will laugh. And no matter how you do, your mother and I will be proud of you."

"Why?" asked Monty. "Why would you be proud if I did something dumb?"

"We'd be proud that you've tried something new this year."

Monty's mother shook her head. "I don't want him to do anything that's going to upset him," she said to her husband.

Monty smiled with relief. "So I don't have to go?" he asked.

"Why don't we go, and you can sit in the back and watch. If you change your mind, you can get up and perform with your classmates," his father suggested.

It was good to know that his parents didn't expect him to take part in the exhibition. Monty relaxed as they drove to the hall. He removed his jacket and took a chair in the back of the room, where the visitors were seated. The twins came over and asked why he wasn't lining up with them.

"Come on," urged Ilene. "We're almost ready to start."

"No," said Monty firmly. "I'm just going to watch tonight."

He walked over and sat by his parents.

Arlene shrugged and ran to take her place among the other students.

Sensei came forward and bowed to the youngsters.

All the children bowed back to him.

The exhibition began. Sensei called some of the older students forward. He asked them to show off some of their skills. Ellie, Clyde, and Kevin did punches, both forward and reverse, and knife-hand punches. Then they began performing kicks. In the midst of a power side kick, Clyde lost his balance and fell down. A few of the children let out giggles, but Sensei looked around the room with a glare. All giggles were muffled at once.

They had been taught that you should never laugh at your opponent. Clyde jumped up and attempted another power side kick. Sensei nodded in approval. This time, Clyde had done it perfectly.

Then Sensei pointed to three other students. Arlene, Ilene, and Charlie moved to the front of the room. As Monty watched them show off their stances and their punches, he began to feel restless. Clyde had fallen down, but he had jumped right back up. If he fell down, he could do the same thing.

Then Sensei was ready to have the next group of students show off their skills. Paul and Jamie came forward. Monty kicked off his shoes and removed his socks. Then he jumped from his seat in the back of the room and stood in line with the two other yellow-belted students. Out of the corner of his eye, Monty recognized Joey sitting in the back row. But instead of wondering how he knew where to come, he concentrated on Sensei Jack's instructions. He bowed with his classmates and listened for directions from the teacher. Together the three karate students showed off their punches and their kicks. They called out in unison, "Kee-yi!"

By the time they were finished, Monty could feel sweat dripping down his neck. Karate was hard work sometimes, but it was fun too. He was glad that he had taken part in the exhibition. And he was very happy that Joey had been there to see him after all.

All the students sat together on one side of the room. Sensei called out some names.

Arlene and Ilene were awarded new purple belts. Then Monty was surprised because Sensei called out his name. He stood and went forward. The teacher handed him a new belt. It was orange.

"Really?" he asked Sensei. "Am I really an orange belt now?"

The teacher nodded and smiled. "You've done the easy ones," he said. "It's going to get harder and harder to move ahead. But if you keep working at it, you can succeed."

"I will, sir," Monty promised his karate teacher. He knew he could do it.

Monty removed his yellow belt and carefully tied the orange one around his waist. It was an amazing thing, but he suddenly realized something. Orange was his favorite color. It was the color of orange juice and the inside of a cantaloupe and sweet potatoes. It was sunsets and sherbet and all sorts of other wonderful things. It was great to have an orange belt.

Monty was mighty pleased with himself.

Don't miss these other stories starring Monty!

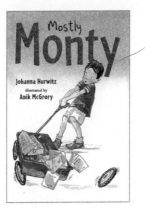

Mostly Monty

Amazing Monty

Johanna Hurwitz
illustrated by Anik McGrory